A PET FOR FLY GUY

Tedd Arnold

SCHOLASTIC INC.

Specially for Scott and McKenzie

ISBN 978-0-545-83105-5

Copyright © 2014 by Tedd Arnold. All rights reserved.
Published by Orchard Books, an imprint of Scholastic Inc.
ORCHARD BOOKS and design are registered trademarks of
Watts Publishing Group, Ltd., used under license.
SCHOLASTIC and associated logos are trademarks and/or
registered trademarks of Scholastic Inc.

12 11 10 9 8 7 6 5 4 3 2   15 16 17 18 19 20/0

Printed in the U.S.A.   40

This edition first printing, January 2015

The display type was hand-lettered.
The text was set in Hank BT.
The art was created digitally using Photoshop.
Book design by Chelsea C. Donaldson

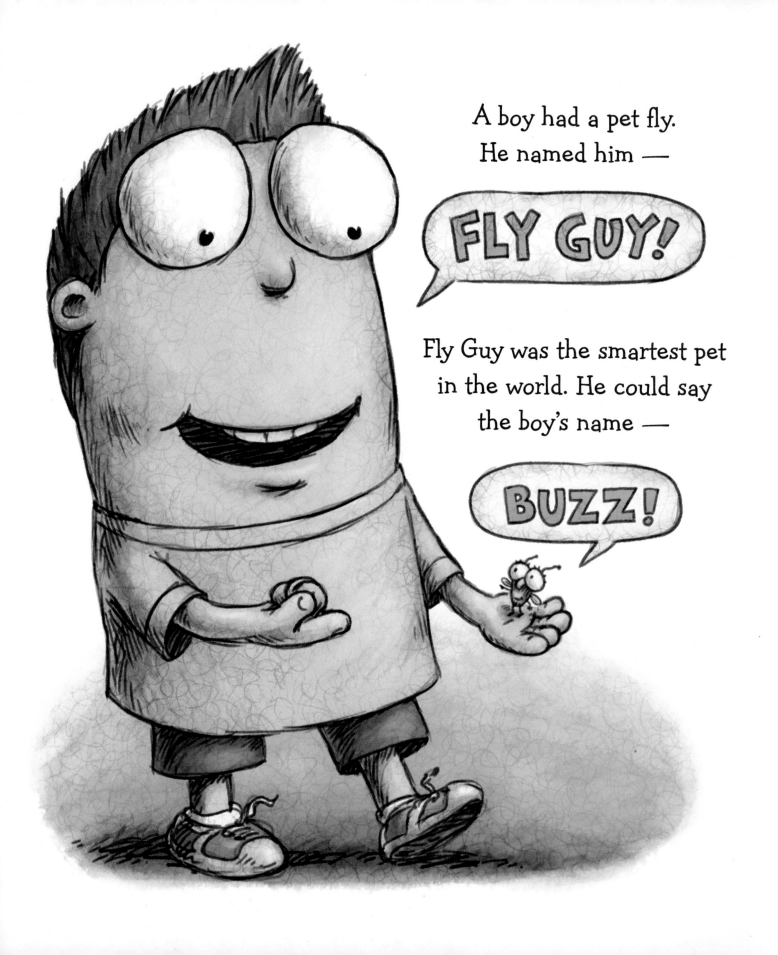

A boy had a pet fly.
He named him —

FLY GUY!

Fly Guy was the smartest pet
in the world. He could say
the boy's name —

BUZZ!

One day, Buzz said,
"Fly Guy, we are going on a picnic!"

Buzz and Fly Guy played chase all the way to the park.

They ate lunch.
They played together.

They looked at clouds.

They watched other people play with their pets.

"Wow!" said Buzz. "Everyone has a pet."

NO PETZ!

"Oops! That's right," said Buzz.
"You don't have a pet."

"But remember, you have to take care of it," said Buzz.

"And play with it," said Buzz.

"And feed it," said Buzz.

"Okay," said Buzz,
"let's go to the
pet shop."

At the pet shop, Buzz came out with a puppy.
It licked Fly Guy.

Buzz came out with a kitten.
It swatted Fly Guy.

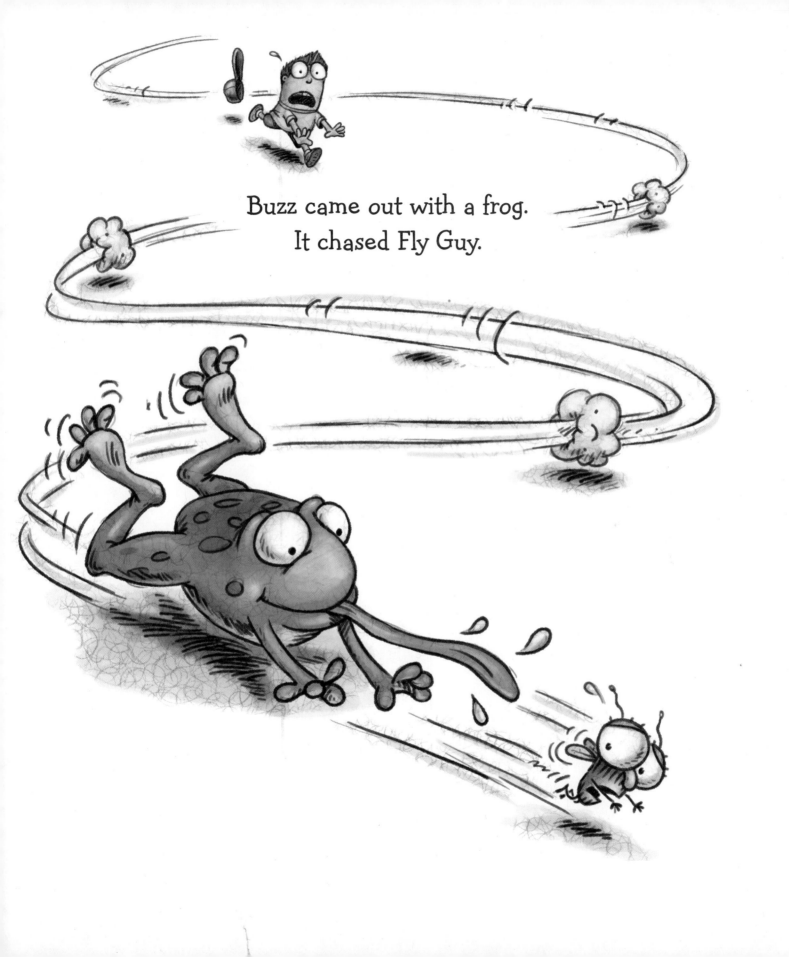

Buzz came out with a frog.
It chased Fly Guy.

Back at the park, Fly Guy found a worm.
It was too slimy.

Fly Guy found a spider.
It was too tangly.

Fly Guy found a cricket.
It was too jumpy.

Buzz said, "Let's think about this whole pet thing."

"You need a pet who
likes to play," said Buzz.
"Just like you."

"You need a pet who can do tricks," said Buzz. "Just like you."

"You need a pet who is a good friend," said Buzz.
"Just like you."

"I never thought of that," said Buzz.
"Okay, sure. I mean, YEZZ!"

"There's just one thing about being your pet," said Buzz.

"You don't have to feed me."

Buzz said, "Do you know who's the best pet
in the whole wide world?"